To: The

Remember —
if you imagine it,
it can happen!

Mary Roberts :)

Once Upon A Monday

By Mary Roberts

Illustrations by Barbara Lipe

Copyright © 2004
Publisher: DinRo
          Naperville, IL

Title: Once Upon A Monday
Author: Mary Roberts
Illustrator: Barbara Lipe
Printed in Hong Kong through Global Interprint, Inc.
1-800-356-1399
First Printing

ISBN 0-9744412-0-1
LCCN: 2003095925

Publisher's CIP Block:
Children's stories—pictorial works.
Imagination—Juvenile fiction.
[E]
3-7 year olds

Summary: A story that highlights a typical day for parent and child, while showing
          the child's imaginative view of the day's activities.

Special Thanks To:
       Jenn and John Roberts for providing me with one of the most wonderful experiences in my life—'being a Mom'
       Barb Lipe for capturing my ideas with her beautiful illustrations
       Mary Ellen Middleton and Scott Etters for their advice and editing assistance
       Minute Man Press and Ray Kinney for their assistance in the early days of this project
       IMS partners Pat, Bob and Lee for their encouragement and technical support in the final stages of the project

In Memory of my father, Henry Dragich III

Long before he became ill, my father encouraged me to write a children's book which he would print in his print shop. Although he would never print my book, it was his spirit and strength that propelled me through this project.

A Note From the Author:

I believe that daily living is full of teachable moments and adventures if we choose to see them. By encouraging the natural curiosity and imagination in children's minds, their potential is unleashed. As my parents taught me, I teach and lead my children to discover the wonders and joy in simple pleasures. There can be fun and magic in everyday life!

I hope that you enjoy reading this book!   I welcome your comments. Please contact me by direct mail or email at mroberts@innovativemodular.com.

At the end of the day, if bedtime came without grumbles and groans, Jennifer could choose a story.

Tonight, she wanted to hear one of Mommy's made-up "Good Little Jennifer" stories about their day. So, she hopped into bed and pulled up the covers.

On this starlit night, Jennifer's mother began her story.

Once upon a Monday,
there was a lively, curious little girl named Jennifer,
who lived in the Kingdom of Neighborville.

This morning, the household was jolted to life as Jennifer jumped out of bed and rushed down the hall to wake her mother.

As Mother struggled to open her eyes,
she heard her daughter's excited voice,
"Are you up, Mommy?
Why does the Sandman like to put sand in my eyes?
What's for breakfast? Why are you still sleeping?"

Peeling her eyes open to the sound of her walking, talking alarm clock, Mommy knew the day had begun.

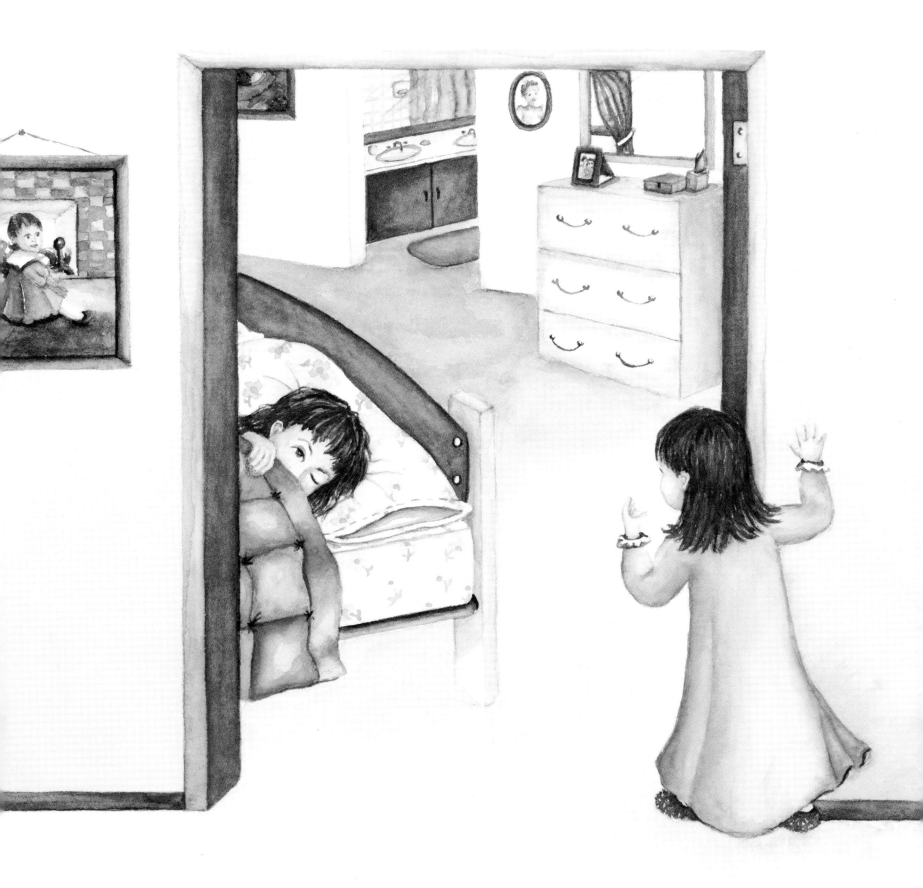

Awake and out of bed, Mommy smiled at her energetic little girl.
She answered the wake-Mom-up questions,
and told Jennifer that they needed to get ready for a busy day.

While drying the breakfast dishes,
Jennifer was bursting with energy and anxious to find out about
their plans.

"C'mon Mommy, you said we had lots to do!
What are we going to do? Where are we going?
Why do we have lots to do?"

Jennifer, of the Kingdom of Neighborville, was a little girl with
lots of questions and a big imagination. Her mother liked that.

Jennifer imagined, *what might happen that day.*

Today, Mommy revealed that they would go to the grocery store, the dry cleaners and the library.

As her other ideas faded away, Jennifer pleaded, "Can we go to the library first? Pleeeease, Mommy."

At the library, Jen and her mother cuddled for a long time while reading Jennifer's favorite books.

This time, Mommy asked the questions.

"How will the prince ever find Cinderella?
Do you think the wolf will blow down the little pigs' brick house?
What might happen if Jack wakes up the giant?
Do you think you could feel a pea under your mattress?
Can you say Rumplestiltskin?"

She dreamed that *the library in the Kingdom of Neighborville was a place filled with princesses, fairies, giants and goblins.*

After checking out books for home, they were off to the next stop.

Jen and her mother walked down the streets of the Kingdom. On the way to the dry cleaners, they looked in store windows and waved to the shopkeepers as they passed.

Once inside, Jennifer made a face and asked,
"Why does this place smell so funny?"

Mommy explained that chemicals used to clean the clothes
made the strange smell.

Still curious, Jen held her nose and watched the clothes
as they moved past her, turned somehow and then disappeared.

As her mother talked to Mr. Dryer, Jen wondered,
Where did the clothes go? Did they magically move?
How did they stop?
What if she followed the shirts, would she disappear?

She wanted answers to all her questions, but forgot them the instant Mr. Dryer gave her a sucker.

Jen wanted to eat the sucker, but Mommy said not until after lunch.
Jennifer's tummy was growling just as her thoughts *turned to food.*

Returning home, Mommy had her own ideas of what they would eat for lunch. Mommy fixed lunch and wrote a list for the grocery store.

Enjoying the last licks of her sucker, Jen was re-energized.
"C'mon Mommy, let's go!"

While Mommy drove, Jen looked out the car window searching
for the familiar grocery store signs in the Kingdom of Neighborville.

"Which store are we going to today? Are we almost there?
Will the lady give me a sticker?"

Mommy smiled, but wondered how many more questions
she would have to answer today.

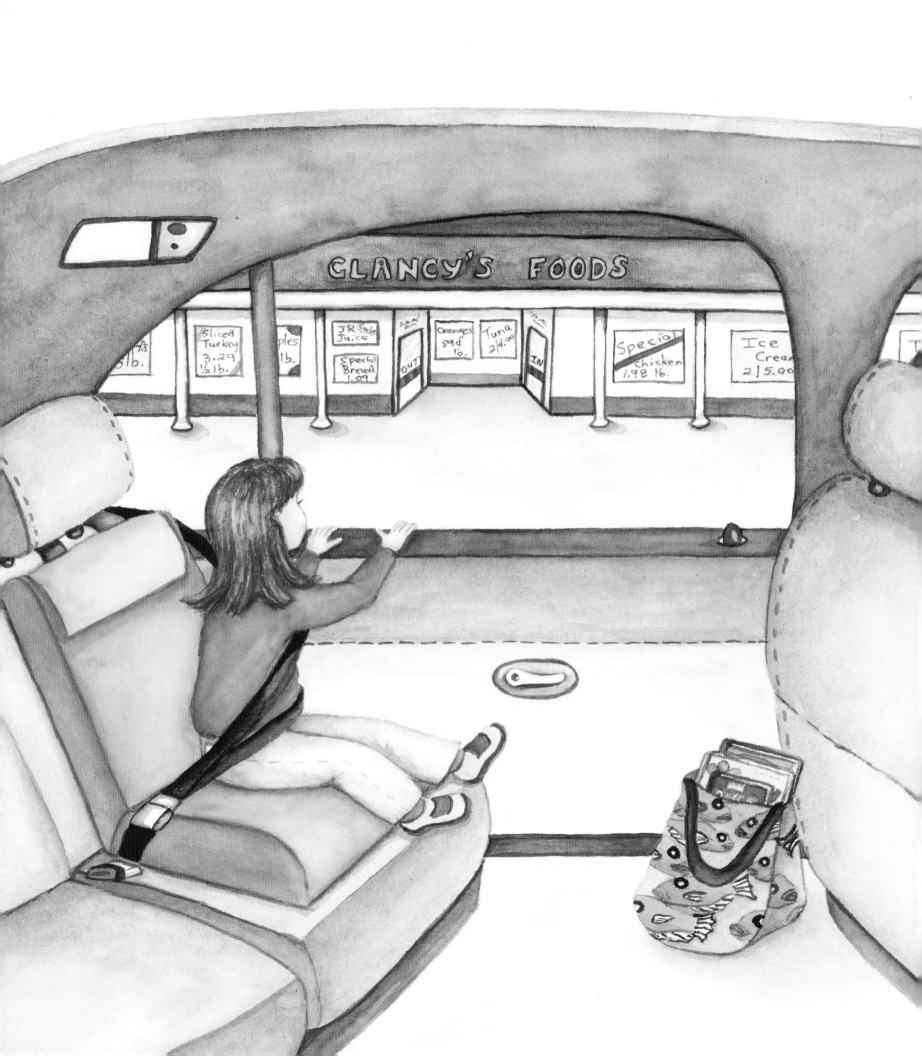

With Jennifer at her side and the grocery list in hand, Mommy walked toward the Produce Section where Jen loved to help pick out fruits and vegetables.

"What's this one, Mommy? Can I squeeze it, too? Can we buy green apples? Why do you like red apples? Why are these bigger?"

Jennifer's mother encouraged her to gently touch the produce, and then explained why she chose each fruit and vegetable.

Mommy placed items in the cart,
as rows of singers on bleachers at church came to Jen's mind.

Jennifer of the Kingdom of Neighborville conducts her own
Chorus of Fruits and Vegetables.

Jen ran to catch up as her mother pushed the cart.
At the Seafood Counter, Jen was most interested in the lobsters.

"How do they get the lobsters out of the tank, Mommy?"

Her mother was asking the grocer to wrap a few salmon steaks,
so replied, "Wait just a minute, please, Jen."

Jen peered closer into the lobster tank *and pretended,*
as she saw Diver Jen being lowered into the tank on a hook.

Jennifer was startled as Mommy pushed the cart into motion again.

She answered Jen's question, explaining that the grocer reaches
in the tank and pulls out the lobsters with his hand.

Moving up and down the aisles Jen asked,
"Do we need cookies? How about candy? Can I pick my own
cereal? Why are some meats red and some white?"

They selected foods as Jennifer continued with the non-stop
questions. Mommy's answers became shorter.

Feeling the sudden cold of the Frozen Foods Section, Mommy
shivered. "Brrrrr..." She liked to hurry through this part of the
store, but it was the aisle of Jennifer's favorite food—ice cream!

"Please, choose a flavor qu-ickly, Jen."

"What kind of ice cream would I like? Hmmm, let me see."

Jen pictured *pleasant penguins presenting delicious desserts.*

She picked mint chocolate chip, and they made their way to the checkout counter.

On the way home, Mommy exclaimed,
"Wow, it's been a busy Monday! You were a big helper.
Thank you for being such a good little Jennifer today."

Jennifer smiled, thought for a moment, and felt happy with her adventures in the Kingdom of Neighborville.

Mommy leaned over and kissed her daughter.

"Oh no, is that the end of the story, Mommy?
Do I have to go to sleep now?"

"Yes, Jennifer."

"But why, Mommy?"

"Because I am tired, and we both need some rest. Tomorrow will
be a new day."

"Good night, Princess Jennifer of the Kingdom of Neighborville.
I love you."

"G'night, Mommy. I love you."

SWEET DREAMS